BEAR IN THE FAMILY

ERIC WALTERS

illustrated by
OLGA BARINOVA

orca Echoes

ORCA BOOK PUBLISHERS

Printed in Canada and the United States in 2022 by Orca Book Publishers.
orcabook.com

Library and Archives Canada Cataloguing in Publication
Title: Bear in the family / Eric Walters ; illustrated by Olga Barinova.
Names: Walters, Eric, 1957- author. | Barinova, Olga, illustrator.
Series: Orca echoes.
Description: Series statement: Orca echoes
Identifiers: Canadiana (print) 20210247061 | Canadiana (ebook) 20210247096 |
ISBN 9781459832978 (softcover) | ISBN 9781459832985 (PDF) | ISBN 9781459832992 (EPUB)
Classification: LCC PS8595.A598 B43 2022 | DDC jC813/.54—dc23

Library of Congress Control Number: 2021941162

Summary: In this partially illustrated early chapter book, a family
return to their home in the forest after a wildfire to find their house
still standing and an orphaned bear cub in the well.

Orca Book Publishers is committed to reducing the consumption of
nonrenewable resources in the production of our books. We make
every effort to use materials that support a sustainable future.

Orca Book Publishers gratefully acknowledges the support for its publishing
programs provided by the following agencies: the Government of Canada,
the Canada Council for the Arts and the Province of British Columbia
through the BC Arts Council and the Book Publishing Tax Credit.

Cover and interior artwork by Olga Barinova
Design by Dahlia Yuen
Edited by Liz Kemp
Author photo by Angelika Langen

Printed and bound in Canada.

25 24 23 22 • 1 2 3 4

Also by Eric Walters:
Batcat and the Seven Squirrels
High and Dry
Hockey Night in Kenya
Prince for a Princess
Skye Above
Saving Sammy

CHAPTER ONE

"Are we almost there?" Jasmin asked.

"It's going to be another thirty minutes at this speed," her father, Sam, answered.

"It's been a pretty slow ride, but there's nothing we can do about it," her mother, Sarah, added.

The family bounced along the rutted road. The grown-ups were in the front seats. Behind them was Tara, who was eight months old and in her car seat, with nine-year-old Jasmin to her right and her seven-year-old brother, Hunter, to her left. The family dog, Brody, was in the very back. Every other available space was full of groceries and supplies.

"I just don't recognize anything," Jasmin said.

"It's so different," her mother agreed.

The familiar trees and landscapes had all been wiped away. All that remained were blackened stumps and trunks and an occasional tree that had somehow survived the forest fire.

"But why is the road so bad?" Jasmin asked.

"The big rains put out the fire, but with the vegetation gone, there was flooding. It caused erosion and wash-outs," her mother explained.

"And speaking of washouts—hold on," their father warned. "I'm going to have to go off-road."

The Jeep bounced into the ditch. He carefully drove around some fallen and burnt trees and then maneuvered back up onto the road.

The drive home from town usually took about forty-five minutes. Town was where they went grocery shopping, where they went to school, where most of their friends lived and where both Jasmin and Hunter were on soccer teams. It was also where their grandparents lived.

For the last two weeks they'd been living at their grandparents' home. Their grandparents were nice, and they loved them, but everyone wanted to get back home. Assuming their home was still there and hadn't been destroyed by the forest fire. The closer they got, the more they worried, because they could see the fire had swept right across the land.

Brody kept leaning over the back seat and putting his head over Jasmin's. She could feel his hot, bad breath, and he drooled a little bit onto her shoulder.

"Brody!" she said as she pushed his head to the side and wiped away the drool with the back of her hand.

Brody leaned down and gave her a lick on the face. She wanted to be mad at him, but she couldn't. He was such a good dog.

Brody had been around longer than the kids. Her parents often joked that he was their original child. When she was little, Jasmin had often taken her naps snuggled around Brody in his big dog bed.

"It really is a beautiful day," her mother said. "The sky is so blue."

It *was* a nice day, and it was good to see the sky and the clouds and the sun. Before the rain had put out the fire, the air had been so filled with smoke at times that the sun was only a brown blur above them. And at night they could see the orange in the sky as the fire burned around them. If it hadn't been so scary, it would have been beautiful.

Thank goodness the town had been spared from the fire. It sat on a lake and was protected on the other side by a rocky hill and the highway. Those things, along with the firefighters, had saved it.

There had been many firefighters in and around the town. They had seemed to be everywhere. They'd worked around the clock, only stopping to sleep and eat before heading back out to continue the fight. They had never even changed out of their firefighting clothes—big black pants, orange vests and helmets. Their faces had always seemed to be smudged. Her parents called them heroes. Everybody did.

There had been firefighters in the sky too. A regular stream of airplanes—water bombers—had landed on the lake, scooped up water and taken off to dump it on the fire.

Now, as Jasmin's family drove, the scenery stayed the same. As far as they could see in every direction, there was nothing but the charred remains of trees. It was just like burnt fingers pointing up toward the sky. No leaves, no color except the blackened trees, the gray rocks and the earth that looked like coal.

"Do you think our house is gone?" Hunter asked.

"If anything survived, it would be our house," their father said.

Their home was made of cement blocks and stone. The roof was metal, and there were metal shutters over all the windows. And although they lived deep in the forest, there were no trees or plants close to the house. There was a large gravel driveway in front, and rock gardens surrounded the house on all sides. Their mother called it a "fire break." She'd designed the whole house to be fire resistant.

"Our house is just over that ridge, right?" Hunter asked.

"I think so. It's hard to tell because everything looks so different," their mom replied.

Hunter reached out and took his sister's hand. They'd know soon enough.

CHAPTER TWO

Their house was just a few turns and hills ahead. *If* it was still there. That was what everybody in the Jeep was thinking but nobody was saying. It felt like they were all holding their breath. And then their driveway came into view.

"The mailbox," Hunter said.

They had had a big wooden mailbox on a pole. It was completely burned away except for part of the pole that was sticking out of the ground.

"It was just a mailbox," their father said.

"I didn't expect it to be there," their mother added.

They turned down the long driveway. Like the road, it was rutted and washed away, and burnt branches had fallen onto it. On both sides the trees had burned away. Their father brought the vehicle to a stop.

"Why are we stopping?" Jasmin asked, looking ahead.

"The bridge is gone," their father answered.

Jasmin clicked off her seat belt and straightened up as high as she could to look out through the windshield. The little bridge that had crossed the narrow drainage ditch was no longer there.

"Now we walk," their mother said.

They all climbed out of the Jeep. As their parents grabbed a few things to carry to the house, Jasmin and Hunter went over to the ditch. There was a bit of water running at the bottom. Brody jumped through the shallow water and bounced up the other side of the ditch.

"Please wait for us," their father called.

He didn't have to ask a second time. Neither of them wanted to go ahead by themselves.

Soon Tara was strapped into a baby carrier against their mother's chest, and everyone crossed over the ditch.

They walked together up the lane toward the house. They went over another little rise in the road, and all of them stopped. What they should have seen there was the barn. What they saw was nothing. The barn had burned to the ground.

"Thank goodness we got all the animals to safety," their mother said.

The five goats and the chickens had come with them to their grandparents' place.

"I guess along with the bridge, we're going to have to make some temporary stalls for the animals before we can bring them back," their mother said.

"Everything will be all right," their father said. "Remember, our house was designed to withstand fire. The barn wasn't."

They'd soon know. It was just around the next curve, behind the rocky hill. The trees on this side of the hill were all gone. Jasmin was almost afraid to go farther. Up until right now she could still believe that the house would be there, that it would have withstood the fire. Now, in a few more seconds and a few more steps, she could find out it was gone.

They reached the top of the hill. The house was there! Their father picked up Hunter and tossed him in the air, Jasmin threw her arms around their mother, and Brody started barking.

"I knew your design would withstand the fire," their father said. "I didn't have a moment's doubt."

Their mother laughed. "I appreciate the faith, but I had my doubts. I made it fire resistant, but no house is fireproof."

They started down the slope, moving faster and faster. And then the sprinklers that surrounded the house came to life. There was a hiss as the water streamed out and the sprinklers turned. The sprinklers

were one of the features their mother had designed to protect the house by keeping it wet.

"It's ten o'clock," their mother said. "The timers are set to go on every hour for ten minutes."

There was a light mist in the air that felt good as they walked closer.

"The house is perfect," Hunter said.

"It looks like it could use a bath," Jasmin added.

The roof of the house, where the sprinklers didn't reach, was covered by a layer of ash. The sprinklers suddenly stopped.

"I thought they were supposed to go for ten minutes," their father said. "Is it possible the well has run dry?"

"I don't think so. I wonder if it's a lack of electricity to run the pump.

Look at the solar panels." Their mother pointed.

The large black panels on the roof were as gray and ash-covered as the rest of the roof.

"I'm surprised the rain didn't rinse off the ashes," their father said. "I'll get up there and clear them off."

They walked toward the front door of the house. It wasn't locked because they never locked their home. Hunter ran forward, getting there first, and pushed the door open. Jasmin was right on his heels, running in after him. They both skidded to a stop just inside the door. With the shutters closed, it was really dark inside. Jasmin reached out and flicked the light switch. The light above their heads hummed and glowed and then faded to nothing.

"Definitely the batteries," their mother said as she tried the lights as well.

There was a loud creaking sound, and the room got much brighter. Their father had opened the metal shutters that protected the large picture window.

Jasmin turned around. Hunter was holding his favorite stuffed animal, Bruno the bear. In the family's rush to leave, somehow Bruno had been left behind. Thank goodness he was here. Thank goodness everything was here.

CHAPTER THREE

"Are you sure you don't want to wait until I can come along?" their father called down from the roof.

His family was below, Tara in the carrier on her mother's chest, and Jasmin and Hunter on the driveway, playing soccer.

"I promised Mr. and Mrs. Jennings that I'd look at their place as soon as I could," their mother replied.

The Jennings were the closest neighbors to the family. They were older than the kids' grandparents. They'd lived in the bush their whole lives and had been the last people to evacuate before the fire swept through. They had temporarily moved south to stay with their oldest daughter and her family. They couldn't come back yet because there were still forest fires burning that cut them off from returning.

"It's not like we can even let them know," he said.

There was no cell-phone reception. The towers had been damaged by the fire. They'd have to travel back into town before they could call anyone.

"I told them I'd go right away. Besides, aren't you curious to find out what happened to their home?" she asked.

"It's probably not going to be good news."

"You can never tell. Fires can burn one place and leave the houses on either side undamaged," she replied.

"We can hope," he said.

"I also think the hike would be good for the kids. It'll take their minds off things."

"I'm not sure how walking through the burned-out forest is going to do that, but it's best to keep them busy," he replied.

"Do you think the kids are doing all right?" she asked.

"They're doing as well as they can. They still have their house."

"I just hope we can tell the Jennings the same," she said.

"We can hope. By the time you get back, we'll have electricity and lights. Just be careful."

"I have bear spray, and we'll take Brody with us," she said.

"I think you're the one protecting Brody these days. I wish he was younger."

"We'll do all right. Just don't you go falling off the roof. See you in a couple of hours."

It was a path they'd traveled often, but now it looked different. There wasn't one tree that wasn't either toppled over or a burned skeleton sticking into the sky. The smell of the fire filled their noses and throats. Normally, Brody would run off into the forest and they would have to keep calling him back. Now he didn't want to go anywhere. Actually, all of them stayed close together on the path.

"This looks like a good place to stop to have a drink," their mother said. "I think the water bottles are in the pack Jasmin's carrying.

Jasmin opened her pack and fumbled around. There were three water bottles, some snacks and two baby bottles filled with milk for Tara. She took a water for everybody and handed them out.

"Here you go, Tara," she said, handing one of the milk bottles to her sister.

Tara took a sip and then tossed it to the ground.

"I guess she's not thirsty," their mother said as she picked it up.

"I'm not that thirsty either, but I want to get rid of the taste of the fire," Jasmin said. She took a long drink.

"Where did all the animals go?" Hunter asked.

"The animals would have run away, and the birds would have flown off," their mother said.

"But there were still chicks in nests. What would have happened to them?" he asked.

"I'm sorry to say they wouldn't have survived the fire," their mother answered.

"But all the other animals got away, right?"

She took a deep breath. "I'm sure most of them got away, but sometimes they get trapped. I'm sorry." She took another drink. "Do you want to rest a little bit longer?"

"Isn't the Jennings place just over this hill?" Jasmin asked.

"Yes. It's just up ahead."

"Then we should go," Hunter answered. "I want to know that their house is all right."

"You two need to understand that it might not be," their mother said.

"But our house was fine," Hunter said.

"Our house was built to be fire resistant. I just want you to be prepared for whatever we find."

They got their packs back on and started moving again. They got to the top of the rise and looked ahead. At first it seemed like they were in the wrong place. It had to be farther ahead. And then Jasmin saw the stone fireplace. It was all that was left. The rest of the house was gone.

CHAPTER FOUR

The log walls of the house had burned down to the stone floor. Everything that had been inside was gone except for a few metal pots sticking out of the ashes, marking where the kitchen had stood.

"I'm so glad they finally agreed to leave," their mother said. "And I know they took all their photo albums and a lot of other personal things with them."

"What now?" Hunter asked.

"I guess they have to decide if they are going to come back and rebuild."

"I meant what now for us. Can we go home?"

"Of course." She looked around. "Where has Brody gone off to?"

"There he is!" Jasmin said.

Brody was over by the well, digging.

"That dog loves to dig. Go and get him," their mother said.

Jasmin ran over. There was already a big hole, and Brody was working to make it bigger. She grabbed him by the collar and started to pull him away. He fought and broke free.

"Brody!" she exclaimed.

He went right back to digging.

She grabbed him again and then heard something. It was very faint, sort of like the wind blowing—no, it was like crying. Was it coming from the hole? She dropped to her knees to listen.

"Jasmin, are you all right?" their mother asked. She and Hunter were now standing behind her.

"Listen," she whispered. "Listen."

Her mother turned her head to the side. "I don't hear—"

And then it came again. It was faint, but it was definitely there.

"It's like crying," Jasmin said. "It almost sounds like Tara."

Tara smiled at the mention of her name. She remained happily held on her mother's chest.

"Is it coming from the well?" Hunter asked.

Jasmin shook her head. "It's coming from the hole *beside* the well. Where Brody was digging."

The hole wasn't very large. It certainly was too narrow for anything bigger than a puppy or a cat.

"The Jennings took their animals with them, right?" Jasmin asked.

"I'm sure they did," their mother said. "But you know their cat, Tiger, likes to go out into the woods."

"You mean they could have left him behind?" Hunter asked.

"Sometimes he'd be gone into the forest for days at a time. What if he was out there and they couldn't wait for him before they had to evacuate?"

Jasmin pictured the Jennings' big old orange cat down in the hole.

"We have to help him! Tiger, come on! Tiger, come out! We're here!" Jasmin cried into the hole, but there was no response.

"Why won't he come out?" Hunter asked.

"He might be scared or even hurt," their mother said.

"We have to help Tiger," Jasmin said.

"I don't know what we can do," their mother said.

The sound came again. It was less a cry than a whimper.

Brody bumped up against the children, shoved them aside and started digging again, kicking the soil out behind him.

"He has the right idea, but we need a shovel," their mother said. She went off to where the toolshed had been. They'd seen some metal tools that had survived the blaze.

Brody stopped digging and looked down the hole. The children crowded in beside him and peered down.

Jasmin saw two glowing, copper-colored eyes looking back at her. They blinked a couple of times. "Tiger, we're here to help you!"

He wasn't any more than two or three feet below the surface. They wouldn't have to dig very much farther to rescue him.

Their mother returned with the metal blade of a shovel. The wooden handle was burned away.

"We see Tiger, Mom. He isn't that far down."

Hunter moved slightly to the side to let their mother see down the hole.

"Something is definitely down there," their mother said. "But I don't know if it's the cat. I wish we had more light before I start digging—wait, there's a flashlight in my pack."

She put down the shovel and looked through her pack, pulling out a flashlight. She aimed it down the hole.

"Oh, my goodness," their mother said.

"It's a bear!" Jasmin gasped. "A little bear cub."

CHAPTER FIVE

As they dug, they were careful not to let dirt fall down onto the bear trapped below. The hole was getting wider and wider. While they worked, Tara crawled on the ground. Her little sleeper was turning gray from the ashes.

As the hole got bigger, they could see the bear cub much more clearly. It was small—their mother thought it would be less than two months old. And it seemed scared.

"Don't be afraid—we're here to help you," Jasmin said, trying to reassure the little bear.

"I can almost reach it now," their mother said.

"How do you think it got down there?" Jasmin asked.

"It might have crawled down there to escape the flames."

"But where's its mother?" Hunter asked.

"They must have been separated by the fire."

Living in the woods, the children had been taught about animals, including bears. They knew that a mother bear would leave its cubs when it went foraging for food. Maybe that's what had happened. The flames of the fire had come between them, and the mother couldn't get back to her cub. And then the fire had driven her away.

"Do you think the mother could still be around, looking for her cub?" Jasmin asked.

Jasmin also knew that getting between a mother bear and its cubs was dangerous.

"If she didn't run far away, she wouldn't have survived the fire," their mother said.

"How long do you think the cub's been down there?" Jasmin asked.

"The fire passed through here three days ago, so at least that long."

Their mother cleared away some more dirt, and a few pieces tumbled down on the little cub. It hardly reacted, like it didn't notice. It was barely moving at all now.

"I think I can get it," their mother said. She lay on the ground and reached down with one arm. "I got it!"

She pulled the bear out and held it up for them to see. It wasn't much bigger than her two hands.

"It's missing fur on a back leg," she said. "I think it was singed off by the fire."

"And its nose is raw," Jasmin added.

The little cub opened its mouth and cried out. Brody barked in answer.

"It must be thirsty and starving," Hunter said. "We can give it some granola or a sandwich."

"It's too young to eat solid food. It wouldn't have been weaned from its mother's milk."

"What about giving it one of Tara's bottles?" Jasmin asked.

"That might work."

Jasmin dug into the backpack and pulled out a bottle. She went to give it to her mother.

"No, you sit down, and I'll hand the bear to you to feed."

Jasmin hesitated.

"It's all right," their mother said. "He's so small and weak. I know you'll be gentle."

Jasmin sat on the top of the well, and her mother gave her the bear. It weighed almost nothing. She took the bottle and placed it by the little bear's mouth. The cub didn't respond.

"Come on, bear, it's milk. You need to drink."

The cub looked up at her. Its eyes were soft and brown. It opened its mouth and gave a weak little cry but still didn't take the bottle.

"Give the bottle a squeeze," their mother said.

Jasmin did, and a few drops of milk dribbled out and into the cub's mouth. It moved its tongue and swallowed. She did it again, with the same result. The cub struggled a bit and then latched on to the bottle.

"It's drinking," Jasmin said, her voice barely a whisper. "It's working."

"That's good. Getting it out of the hole was only the first step in keeping it alive. This is the second."

"And what's the third?" Hunter asked.

"We have to get it home and get some help."

The cub took the entire bottle. He seemed more alive now, and when they put him down, he was able to walk a little. He seemed stronger. They'd also taken some of Tara's diaper cream and put in on the bear's nose, covering the rawness with a film of white.

Hunter picked up the cub. It was even smaller than his stuffed bear, Bruno. Jasmin's bag had been emptied into Hunter's. Her pack was going to be a baby carrier for the bear. Their mother slipped it on Jasmin's front and did up the snaps behind her back.

"Hunter, put the cub in."

He placed him in the pack so that only the bear's head was peeking out the top. Jasmin carefully did up the zipper to hold him in place. The cub struggled a bit but quickly settled in.

"You're just like Kanga and Roo," Hunter said.

"What should we call him?" Jasmin asked.

"Since he's a black bear, we could call it Coal," Hunter said.

"He's too cute and fluffy to be a piece of coal," Jasmin replied.

"It should at least start with the letter *b*," Hunter said. "Like my bear, Bruno."

"That makes sense," their mother said. "And maybe it should have something to do with the fire. Any ideas?"

Jasmin started thinking, and then it came to her. "How about Boo-Boo, because he was left here by mistake?"

"Perfect!" their mother said.

"I like it too," Hunter agreed.

Tara had nothing to say about it, but she did smile.

"Then that's it. Hello, Boo-Boo the Bear."

Boo-Boo looked up, opened his mouth and squeaked out his agreement.

CHAPTER SIX

"I'm seeing it, but I still can't believe it," their father said.

Boo-Boo was wrapped in a pink blanket in Jasmin's arms. He was snuggled up with Bruno the stuffed bear and was taking another bottle. It was his fourth bottle since they'd gotten home. Jasmin had given him all four bottles. He didn't want to feed from anybody else. The little bear had his paws wrapped around the bottle, nails digging in, and was eating greedily. For such a little bear, his claws were already long and sharp.

Boo-Boo drank the last drops. As Jasmin tried to pull the bottle away, he dug his claws in and started complaining loudly, trying to stop her.

"Somebody has a strong opinion," their father joked.

"It's not just his opinion that's getting stronger," their mother said.

She took the bear from Jasmin's arms and carefully unwrapped the blanket. She set the bear on the floor. He stood on his own, but he was still a bit wobbly. And then he started running! He went straight across the room to where Brody was lying in his dog bed and bumped right into him. Brody startled but couldn't be bothered to move. They all cheered and laughed as Boo-Boo burrowed into Brody's side.

"Boo-Boo thinks Brody is his mommy," Hunter said.

"I think it's Brody *and* Jasmin," their mother said. "He likes to snuggle with Brody, but she's the one who's been giving him the bottles. He'll want to be back with her when he gets hungry again."

"Speaking of hungry, my stew is all ready to go," their father said.

"Can I eat here instead of in the kitchen?" Jasmin asked.

"I think we can all eat here," their mother said.

Hunter, Jasmin and their mother settled in around the coffee table while their father went to get them supper. Tara had already been put to sleep for the night. Their father returned with a tray holding four bowls of steaming stew. It smelled delicious.

Along with making dinner, he had brought up all the groceries and cleaned off the solar panels. The lights were shining brightly. It all seemed so normal that it was easy for everybody to forget what had happened all around them. The only reminder inside the house was the little bear.

"Where's Boo-Boo going to sleep tonight?" Jasmin asked.

"He can sleep in my bed," Hunter offered.

"I'm pretty sure he's going to want to stay cuddled up with Brody," their mom said.

"Brody is the closest thing he has to his mother," their father said.

"Dad, do you think she'd come looking for her baby?" Jasmin asked.

"I think she's either far, far away or..." He let the sentence trail off.

"Or dead, right?" Hunter asked.

He slowly nodded his head. "Sorry, but I don't know how anything could have survived the fire."

"Boo-Boo did," Jasmin pointed out.

"He is one lucky little bear to have lived through that," their father said. "So tell me what you two know about black bears."

"They're called black bears, but sometimes they have brown fur," Jasmin said.

"And lots of them have a little bit of white fur on the chest, like Boo-Boo does," Hunter added.

Boo-Boo had a little crescent of white on his chest.

"Are they dangerous?" their father asked.

"They're wild animals, so they can be dangerous," Jasmin said.

"Especially when they're protecting their babies," Hunter added.

"That's like all mothers," their mother stated.

"But generally, if you leave them alone, they leave you alone," Jasmin said.

"That's a good thing. Look at the claws on him and think about an animal as big as me with paws the size of dinner plates," their father said. "What do they eat?"

"They eat everything," Hunter said.

"You mean like rocks and trees?" Jasmin asked jokingly.

"You know what I mean. They eat plants and insects and even other animals. Small animals," he replied. "Not people-sized animals."

"But mainly they eat plants, like seeds and berries. I think more than 90 percent of their diet is plants," Jasmin added.

"And they eat a lot in the summer and fall so they can hibernate in the winter," Hunter said.

"Winter is also when they have their babies," Jasmin said. "How old do you think Boo-Boo is?"

"It's just a guess, but I think less than three months," their father replied.

"How long will it be until he can eat food, not just milk?" Jasmin asked.

"It will be at least four or five months before he's weaned," he replied.

"When that happens, we'll get him seeds and berries and lots of other stuff," Hunter said.

"That won't be anything we'll have to worry about," their mother answered.

"Why not?" Hunter asked.

"Well, he's only going to be with us tonight."

"What?" both Hunter and Jasmin exclaimed together.

"We can't raise a bear," their father said.

"Why not?" Jasmin asked.

"Yeah, why not?" Hunter echoed.

"Because he's a wild animal who will grow up to be a very big bear," their mother answered. "That's why we can't keep him."

"But he'll die if we let him go! We have to keep him!" Jasmin pleaded.

"Oh goodness, we're not talking about letting him go," their mother said. "But we need to take him someplace where he can be properly cared for."

"We can care for him!" Hunter protested. "We'll take good care of him, the way we do with Brody. Honestly."

Hunter looked like he was on the verge of tears.

"Come here, big guy," his father said to him. Hunter went over to his dad, who put an arm around his shoulders. "You and Jasmin take great care of Brody."

"And we know you'll take great care of our next pet," their mother added. "But Boo-Boo is not a pet."

"Would you rather have him live out his life in the wild or in a cage?" their father asked.

"In the wild," Jasmin said.

"Being in the forest," Hunter replied.

"There are people who know how to raise cubs so they can go back into the wild. Doesn't Boo-Boo deserve that?" their mother asked.

They both nodded their heads.

"Maybe he can even find his mother," Hunter said.

"Tomorrow we'll drive into town and talk to Dr. Gleason, who runs the animal shelter," their mother said.

"But isn't the shelter for dogs and cats?" Jasmin asked.

"It is, but he'll know who we have to contact," their father said. "I hope you two will come with me. I think Boo-Boo would like that."

"I'll come," Jasmin said.

"Me too," Hunter agreed.

"And for tonight we'll take care of Boo-Boo," their mother said. "Me, your father, the two of you and, of course, Brody."

CHAPTER SEVEN

Their father moved quietly to try not to wake anybody. Boo-Boo, Brody and Jasmin were all curled up in Brody's dog bed on the floor. They were sleeping now, but they'd been up four times in the night. Baby bears were just like baby humans and needed to be fed every few hours.

Sam pulled out his phone. The three of them made a very cute picture.

He checked his phone again to see if he had any reception. There were still no bars.

"Good morning," Sarah said quietly as she entered the room. She was carrying Tara. "How did you sleep?"

"I was up four times," he said. "That is one hungry little bear. Jasmin got up each time and fed him the bottle."

"They look so cute. You should take some pictures."

He held up his phone. "Already done."

"How soon are you going to leave?" she asked.

"Right after breakfast. I want to get some lumber to put in a new bridge over the ditch."

"Can you also call the Jennings to let them know?"

He let out a big sigh. "I'll let them know."

"Thank you. I'll go make breakfast. You should try to get a little bit of shut-eye before you go."

Just then Boo-Boo called out. Jasmin heard his call and woke up. The little bear bumped into her, rubbing his face against hers.

"Good morning, Boo-Boo. I guess it's time for another bottle."

"And soon it'll be time to get going," her father said. "If for no other reason than to get more milk. We're almost out."

The back seat of the car was shared by Jasmin, Hunter and Brody. Boo-Boo, along with Bruno, was in a little cardboard box nestled in between the two children. Every time Boo-Boo made a sound, Brody leaned over Jasmin so he could nuzzle and lick the little cub.

"Are we going to stop in at Grandma and Grandpa's?" Hunter asked.

"Of course. Right after we take care of Boo-Boo. Speaking of that, we're here."

They pulled into the parking lot of the animal shelter. They could hear dogs barking. Brody stuck his head out the window and barked back.

Jasmin picked up Boo-Boo and wrapped him in a blanket. She offered him another bottle. He grabbed it with his paws and started drinking instantly.

"Brody has to wait here," their father said. "He'll be fine with all the windows down."

They got out and walked toward the building and the barking. As they got to the door, Jasmin hesitated and took a deep breath. She knew this was the right thing to do, but it was hard. They walked in, and there was Dr. Gleason, the veterinarian, sitting behind the counter.

"Hey, George," their father said.

"Sam. Good to see you and the kids."

"Hello, Dr. Gleason," both children said.

"Sam, your home—is it okay?" he asked.

"The barn burned to the ground, but the house is fine. I wish I could say the same about the Jennings' place."

"It's sad that so many homes were lost and so many people had to evacuate. Some couldn't even take their pets with them. On top of it all, we've had three dogs have litters in the last few weeks. It's a full house."

"I can hear that. Do you have space for one more?"

"We always make space. So what do you have for me, a kitten?"

All he could see was the bottle and the tip of Boo-Boo's nose, covered with white diaper cream.

"Show him, Jasmin."

She peeled back the blanket.

"Oh, my goodness, a bear cub!" he exclaimed. "Let me have a closer look."

Dr. Gleason took the cub from Jasmin and unwrapped the blanket. Boo-Boo objected a little bit, crying out before going back to his bottle. As the vet examined him, they explained the whole story about finding Boo-Boo.

"Other than a little singed fur on the back leg and a burnt nose, he seems healthy. You've done a great job."

"It was mainly Jasmin," Hunter said.

"You helped," she replied.

"I'm not equipped to provide care for a bear cub, especially not one this young," Dr. Gleason said. "I just don't have the staff to do it."

"We thought you might know who could care for it," their father said.

Dr. Gleason handed Boo-Boo back to Jasmin. "You wait here while I make a couple of phone calls."

"We have Brody out in the car, so we'd better wait outside," their father said.

"Probably better," Dr. Gleason said. "Besides, I think all the barking is a bit disturbing to your little bear."

Brody barked excitedly when he saw them coming. Hunter ran ahead and opened the back door. Brody bounded out of the car and ran toward Jasmin. He jumped up, practically knocking Jasmin over as he got on his back legs and nuzzled Boo-Boo.

"I think somebody is happy to see Boo-Boo again," their father said.

Jasmin almost said, *Then he's going to be pretty sad soon.* But she knew Brody wasn't the only one who was going to be sad. In a few minutes Dr. Gleason was going to come and take Boo-Boo from them. Just as Jasmin was thinking this, the door of the shelter opened and the vet came out.

"I got a hold of someone," Dr. Gleason said. "I have some good news, some bad news and a question."

"That pretty well covers every possibility," their father said. "So?"

"The good news is that the bear-rescue people have the perfect place to provide care, and they'll send somebody to get your bear."

"And the bad news?" their father asked.

"They won't be able to come for two or more weeks," he said.

"Why so long?"

"The fires that swept through the region have left a lot of abandoned and injured wild animals. They're as overwhelmed as we are. As well, we're still cut off from them by fires that are still burning."

"What happens to Boo-Boo in the meantime?" their father asked.

"That's the question part. He needs a foster home until they can come up to get him, and they were wondering if—"

"We'll keep him!" Jasmin exclaimed.

"Sam?" Dr. Gleason asked.

Sam turned to Jasmin and Hunter. "You two know it's going to be a lot of work and a lot more getting up in the middle of the night," their father said.

"We'll do it, we'll do it, I promise!" Jasmin said, and Hunter nodded in agreement.

Their father smiled. "We'll take him."

Jasmin and Hunter and Brody started dancing around.

CHAPTER EIGHT

There was a loud crash, and Jasmin's eyes popped open. Immediately there was a scrabbling of claws on the floor. Jasmin didn't know what Boo-Boo had done, but it sounded bad. She rolled off the sofa and saw that the metal bowl was on the floor, sitting amid scattered apples and oranges. That cub could cause so much trouble. He had to be watched all the time.

Boo-Boo came running back toward her, crying. It was his "feed me, I'm hungry" cry.

He bumped into her leg and then started to climb up her pajamas.

"Boo-Boo, that hurts!" she screamed as his nails went through the material and into her leg.

She picked him up, and he nuzzled her face. Even when he was annoying, he was cute. She carried him over to the counter, where there was a bottle waiting.

"Good morning, Jasmin," her mother said. She was carrying Tara. "How did your night go?"

Jasmin held up three fingers. "I was up feeding him three times, and he's hungry again."

"I was up twice with this one last night, and she's hungry again too. Now you know what it's like to be a parent."

"I'm just glad I don't have to do this every night."

Jasmin and her father had been taking turns for the ten days Boo-Boo had been with them. They'd quickly come to realize how much work it was to raise a cub. Along with the nighttime feedings, he had to be watched all the time. Between knocking things over, climbing the curtains and clawing at the sofa, he also wanted to put everything in his mouth.

So much of what he did reminded Jasmin of caring for Tara. Of course, Tara didn't climb the curtains. At least, not yet.

"I think that cub grew overnight," her mother said.

"Dad weighed him yesterday. He's almost twice as big as he was when we found him."

Boo-Boo finished the bottle and started complaining. "Go and find Brody," Jasmin said as she put him down.

Boo-Boo ran off, tumbled over and skidded across the floor. He got back up and started crying. This was a different sound—he was calling for Brody.

Brody heard the call and trotted into the room. Boo-Boo nuzzled his side, and the dog began licking him.

Their father came into the room, holding up his phone. "We have cell-phone reception! The towers are back up!"

Everybody let out a cheer. That meant the internet would be working again as well.

"That's great. I want to talk to my parents, and I should call the Jennings to see how they're doing," their mother said.

Sam had called the Jennings the day he and the kids were in town and given them the bad news, but their mother hadn't had a chance to tell them herself how sorry she was.

"I also want to call the bear-rescue people to tell them how Boo-Boo's doing and see if there's an update," their father said.

Both Jasmin and Hunter were going to be sad to see Boo-Boo go, but they had accepted that they couldn't raise him. Even at this age, his nails were like razors and his teeth like needles.

At that instant Brody yelped and jumped to his feet—probably Boo-Boo's nails at work.

"Come on, Brody, come on, Boo-Boo, let's go for a walk!" Jasmin called out.

"I'll go with you," Hunter added.

"Breakfast will be ready when you get back," their father said.

Jasmin held the door, and Brody, Boo-Boo and Hunter ran outside. She couldn't help smiling as she watched the little bear run and stumble, fall over and get back up as he raced after Brody.

"He is so cute, but he's so much work," Jasmin said.

"I could stay up and feed him one night," Hunter offered.

"Thanks, but it's not going to be that many more nights."

"I'm going to miss him."

"Me too," Jasmin agreed. "But it's better for him."

"I know. It's just...don't you wish he could stay?"

"Sometimes," she admitted. "But they'll take good care of him. They know how to raise baby bears."

"And how to release him back into the wild," Hunter added.

"That's the most important thing."

Their father came out of the house and walked over to them.

"You two have been such good bear parents," he said.

"We've been trying," Jasmin replied.

"I know he'll never forget you." He paused. "I just spoke to the bear-rescue society. They're going to come and pick him up tomorrow."

"Couldn't they wait and come in a week or two?" Hunter asked.

"They said the sooner the better for Boo-Boo. He'll be in a pen with other cubs. He needs to bond with bears instead of people and Brody."

"Brody is going to miss him," Jasmin said.

"We're all going to miss him," their father said. "And I think he's going to miss us."

CHAPTER NINE

Everyone was quiet on the drive out to the highway to meet the bear-rescue people. Boo-Boo had finished a bottle and then snuggled into Jasmin the way he always did after he'd been fed. Jasmin thought about how this was the last bottle she'd ever give him.

"There they are," their father called out.

Jasmin saw a truck with the words *Bear Rescue* and pictures of bears on the side. A man and a woman stood beside it.

Their father stopped beside the truck. "You both ready?" he asked.

"We're ready," Hunter replied, and Jasmin nodded. She thought if she talked right now, she might cry. Boo-Boo was wrapped in his little pink blanket. She picked him up, and they all got out of the Jeep. Brody whined as they walked away.

"Can Brody come?" Hunter asked.

Their father nodded. "I think he wants to say goodbye too."

Hunter ran back to get him.

"Hello!" the woman called out. "You must be the Williams family."

"Yes, hello," their father replied.

They introduced themselves. The man bent down and gave Brody a big pat, and Brody licked his face in return. The man laughed, and that made Jasmin feel better.

"And I'm assuming that's our bear in the blanket," the woman said.

Jasmin wanted to say it was *her* bear, but she didn't.

"Can I hold him?" the woman asked.

Jasmin hesitated.

"I know this is hard," she said. "When we finally release them into the wild, we know it's the right thing to do, but it's always hard to say goodbye."

That was exactly what Jasmin needed to hear. That's why they were doing this.

She nodded. Gently the woman took Boo-Boo in her arms. She peeled back the blanket.

"He's younger than we thought," the man said.

The woman placed Boo-Boo on the ground. He struggled to get away, but she held him in place. He was trying to get to Brody. Instead, Brody moved in close to him.

"These two seem pretty close," the man said.

"They are. Boo-Boo's pretty attached to Brody and to Jasmin," their father said.

"It's great that he's made attachments. Soon enough he'll have other bears to bond with," the man said.

"I just want to examine him," the woman explained. "He's very lively, good weight, bright eyes, nose is cold and wet.

Did he have some fur back here that got singed in the fire?"

"Yes, plus his nose was burned," their father explained.

"His nose looks great. Actually, everything looks great."

Hearing that made Jasmin happy.

"Cubs this young hardly ever survive without their mother. You all did a great job," the man said.

"And we promise to keep up that good work," the woman added.

"Thank you," their father said. "That's all we want. It's just hard to say goodbye."

"You can call anytime you want, and we'll update you on his progress," the man said.

"Really?" Jasmin asked.

The man nodded. "He's in our care now, but you're still part of the team."

"Team Boo-Boo the bear," the woman added.

"Thanks for saying that," their father said.

"Thank you for all you've done," she replied. "Now we have to get going. We have a long drive ahead of us."

"We have one more bottle. Do you want to take it?" Jasmin asked.

"We have some bottles made up, but I'm sure Boo-Boo would like that one too," the man said.

Jasmin ran off to get the bottle, and Hunter ran after her. She picked up the bottle, and Hunter picked up Bruno. Hunter had been cuddling Bruno the whole drive there.

They returned, and she handed the man the bottle.

"I think Bruno should go with Boo-Boo," Hunter said as he held out the bear.

"But he's your favorite stuffed animal!" their father exclaimed.

"He's Boo-Boo's favorite too. He needs him more than I do."

"Are you sure?" their father asked, and Hunter nodded.

"We'll take care of *both* bears," the man said as he took Bruno.

"How about if you carry Boo-Boo to the truck?" the woman asked Jasmin.

She picked up Boo-Boo. He instantly nuzzled her shoulder.

"He's going to miss you," the woman said.

"We're going to miss him," Jasmin said.

Just then Brody bounced up onto his back legs so he could put his face right by Boo-Boo's face. The two licked each other.

The rescue people climbed into their truck, and Jasmin handed the bear to the woman. Boo-Boo snuggled into both her and Bruno. Hunter knew he'd done the right thing in letting Bruno go with him.

"If you call tonight, we'll let you know how he's settling in," the woman said.

"We'll do that," their father replied.

They closed their doors, and the truck started with a rumble. The man honked the horn, and the woman waved goodbye as they drove away.

Their father put an arm around Jasmin and Hunter. Brody pushed in against them too. They watched as the truck got smaller and smaller, and then they couldn't see it anymore.

"How are you two feeling?"

"Sad and happy," Jasmin said.

"Me too," Hunter agreed. "I'm going to miss him."

"I'm going to miss him too," their father said.

"But it will be great to be able to sleep through the night again," Jasmin said.

"Well, I'm thinking that still might be a problem," their father replied.

"What do you mean?" Jasmin asked.

"I could tell you, but I think it would be better to show you," their father said. "And there he is, right on time."

A car pulled up right beside them. Jasmin recognized Dr. Gleason, the veterinarian. He got out of the car. He was holding something. It was small and furry and black.

"It's a puppy!" Hunter exclaimed.

"It's *our* puppy," their father said.

Both kids squealed with joy and ran toward Dr. Gleason. He handed the puppy to Jasmin.

"We thought Brody needed some-body to play with," he said. "But you know that puppies are a lot of work."

"As much as bear cubs?" Jasmin asked.

"Almost."

"We'll help! We promise!" Jasmin said. "And Brody will help too."

"I'm counting on it," he replied. "Do you have any idea what you're going to call him?" Dr. Gleason asked.

"I have an idea," Jasmin said. "What about Bear?"

"Yes, can we call him Bear?" Hunter asked.

Their father replied with a smile and a nod.

Jasmin pulled the puppy close to her face. "Welcome to the family, little Bear. We promise to take good care of you."

AUTHOR'S NOTE

Jasmin and Hunter and their family are characters in a story I wrote to introduce young readers to wildlife-rehabilitation centers like the one that takes in Boo-Boo. In real life, you should never approach a wild animal, even one that looks injured or alone. Keep your distance, and contact a wildlife-rehabilitation center or conservation officer in your area if you think the animal needs help. In my travels throughout Canada, I've had the opportunity to visit some of these centers, including the Northern Lights Wildlife Shelter just outside Smithers, British Columbia. Staff there devote their lives to caring for injured and abandoned wild animals. Over the last thirty-one years, the shelter has taken in 563 bears, 112 moose calves, 156 deer fawns and hundreds of smaller mammals and birds, which the staff raised, rewilded and released back into the wild. Go to wildlifeshelter.com to find out more and donate to allow the shelter to keep doing its important work.

ERIC WALTERS is a Member of the Order of Canada and the author of over 115 books that have collectively won more than 100 awards, including the Governor General's Literary Award for *The King of Jam Sandwiches*. A former teacher, Eric began writing as a way to get his fifth-grade students interested in reading and writing. Eric is a tireless presenter, speaking to over a hundred thousand students per year in schools across the country. He lives in Guelph, Ontario.

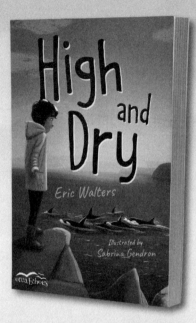
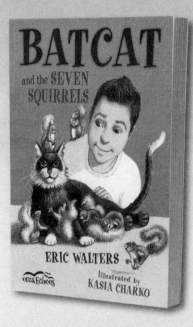